Dear Parent:
Your child's love of reading starts here!

Every child learns to read in a different way and at his or her own speed. Some go back and forth between reading levels and read favorite books again and again. Others read through each level in order. You can help your young reader improve and become more confident by encouraging his or her own interests and abilities. From books your child reads with you to the first books he or she reads alone, there are I Can Read Books for every stage of reading:

SHARED READING
Basic language, word repetition, and whimsical illustrations, ideal for sharing with your emergent reader

BEGINNING READING
Short sentences, familiar words, and simple concepts for children eager to read on their own

READING WITH HELP
Engaging stories, longer sentences, and language play for developing readers

READING ALONE
Complex plots, challenging vocabulary, and high-interest topics for the independent reader

I Can Read Books have introduced children to the joy of reading since 1957. Featuring award-winning authors and illustrators and a fabulous cast of beloved characters, I Can Read Books set the standard for beginning readers.

A lifetime of discovery begins with the magical words "I Can Read!"

Visit www.icanread.com for information
on enriching your child's reading experience.

For Staci, whose wonderful
staff helped instill a love of
reading in my kids
—A.L.

I Can Read® and I Can Read Book® are trademarks of HarperCollins Publishers.

Chicken on a Broom
Copyright © 2019 by HarperCollins Publishers
All rights reserved. Printed in the United States of America. No part of this book may be used or reproduced in any manner whatsoever without written permission except in the case of brief quotations embodied in critical articles and reviews. For information address HarperCollins Children's Books, a division of HarperCollins Publishers, 195 Broadway, New York, NY 10007.
www.icanread.com

Library of Congress Control Number: 2018961831
ISBN 978-0-06-236422-7 (trade bdg.)—ISBN 978-0-06-236421-0 (pbk.)

Typography by Marisa Rother

19 20 21 22 23 LSCC 10 9 8 7 6 5 4 3 2 1

❖
First Edition

n Read!

READING

CHICKEN
on a BROOM

By Adam Lehrhaupt
Pictures by Shahar Kober

HARPER
An Imprint of HarperCollinsPublishers

Zoey and Sam put on their costumes.
They were heading to the party
when Sam noticed Pip.

Pip looked upset.

5

"What's wrong, Pip?" asked Sam.

"My mask is in the barn," said Pip.

"So?" asked Sam.

"The barn is haunted!" said Pip.
"There's a ghost, a huge spider,
and a vampire in there, too.".

"Not a problem," said Zoey.

"Sam and I will help get your mask."

"You will?" asked Pip.

"We will?" asked Sam.

"Keep your hat on, Sam," said Zoey.

"This chicken rides a broom."

"Henry, want to help?" asked Zoey.

"Pip's mask was stolen by ghosts."

"No thanks," said Henry.

"I'm setting up for the party.

Good luck with that ghost."

"Clara, want to help?" asked Zoey.

"Pip's mask was stolen by ghosts."

"Ghosts?" asked Clara.

"There's no such thing."

"I hope that's true," said Sam.

"Don't worry," said Zoey.

"The broom and I will protect you."

"It's very dark in there," said Sam.

"Maybe we should come back later."

"Not a problem," said Zoey.

"This broom is fully equipped!

It comes with a flashlight!"

"Where's the mask?" asked Zoey.

"It's in the loft," said Pip.

"Okay, let's go
up the stairs," said Zoey.
"What about the ghost?" asked Sam.
But Zoey was already off.

The wind howled through the loft.

WOOOOO!

"I'm scared," said Pip.

"It's just the wind," said Sam.

"Not the wind," said Zoey.

"Ghosts!"

"Help!" said Pip.

"Don't let them eat me!" said Sam.

"Abra-kazoom!

Meet my broom!" said Zoey.

Zoey swept the ghosts aside.

"Watch out, Pip," said Sam.

"You have hay on your head."

"Not hay," said Zoey.

"Cobwebs!

Abra-kazoom! Meet my broom!"

Zoey swept the cobwebs aside.

"What's in that cobweb?" asked Sam.

"AHHH!" squeaked Pip.

"It's a giant spider!"

"Not a spider," said Zoey.

"Pip's mask!"

"My mask!" said Pip.

"Can we go now?" asked Sam.

"We can go," said Zoey.

"We just need to avoid that bat!"

"A baseball bat?" asked Sam.

"Not a baseball bat," said Zoey.

"A dangerous vampire bat!

ABRA-KA-RUN!"

Everyone ran.

"That was close," said Zoey.

"Everyone okay?"

Everyone was.

"Can we go to the party?" asked Pip.

"Can we get some treats?" asked Sam.

"We can do both," said Zoey.

"Let's go!"

"You found your mask," said Henry.

"We did!" said Pip.

"The spider had it, not the ghost!"

"We should get a reward," said Sam.

"Maybe some treats?"

"Not just treats," said Zoey.

"Bobbing for apples!" said Zoey.

"YUM!" said Sam.

"Me first, me first!"